The Moonshadow Cat Race

ATTACKED BY A SEA MONSTER. GO BACK TO 27

FLY LIKE A BIRD AND GO TO 52

CHASED BY A CROCODILE. GO BACK TO 44

MOONSHADOW

IDEA AND PAINTINGS BY

Justin Todd

TEXT BY

ANGELA CARTER

LONDON · VICTOR GOLLANCZ LTD · 1982

Idea and paintings © Justin Todd 1982/Text © Angela Carter 1982
Printed in Italy by A. Mondadori Editore, Verona

British Library Cataloguing in Publication Data
Todd, Justin
Moonshadow.
I. Title II. Carter, Angela
823'. 914[J]   PZ7
ISBN 0-575-03026-7

Tom always closed his eyes and pretended to go to sleep when Mother tucked him up and put out the light but as soon as the door closed behind her he was wide awake, again. Now his real, exciting life began, when the wall beside his bed was white with moonlight and Tom was alone with his shadow.

Shadows are never what they seem. They have no shapes of their own, only the shapes we give them. Tom could turn his shadow into marvellous animals, one animal after another. His shadow never knew what Tom would turn it into, next. It never got a moment's rest. It complained to the Man in the Moon.

One night, just as Tom had turned his shadow into a cat, a white, shining gnome jumped in through his window and landed with a thud on the bed. Tom was so startled he forgot about his shadow. His shadow was stranded on the wall, muttering.

'I'm the Man in the Moon!' announced the shining gnome. 'Your shadow wants you to know it's sick and tired of the tricks you make it play. It's high time it had a little holiday.'

The Man in the Moon peeled Tom's shadow off the wall as if it were old wallpaper. The moonshadow cat jumped down onto the floor, shook itself, and looked around. Just then, a mouse happened out of its hole and the moonshadow cat could not resist it— off after the mouse it sped!

TOM WENT SCRAMBLING AFTER THEM

Out of the front door ran the moonshadow cat and Tom ran outdoors, too. In the dark garden, the other shadows rustled and whispered together: 'Here comes the boy who overworked his shadow!'

Shrubs and flowers watched and laughed to see Tom tumble along behind the moonshadow cat on the road to town. The town was fast asleep and snoring. The moonshadow cat, safely camouflaged, looked back over its shoulder and chuckled.
Its holiday had started well.

When they reached the wild wood, the trees woke up,
yawned, stretched and picked the moonshadow cat
up in their gnarled arms, to hide him. Tom was out of
breath from running. His heart went pit-a-pat when
the trees twitched at his pyjamas with twiggy fingers
and tugged him this way and that way. He saw
shadows everywhere but nowhere could he see his
own shadow.

At last an old oak took pity on Tom and said in its creaking voice: 'Your moonshadow cat made off, young Tom, but my friend the mountain can help you look for him. Let me introduce you both.'

The mountain picked Tom up in his stony hand and held him high in the air. Tom scanned around and around and – there it was! His moonshadow cat, clinging to a cliff only a giant's stride or so away. Only a giant's stride…but Tom was no giant.

'Well, I *am* a giant,' said the mountain
and stretched his long legs. But when
the quick, clever moonshadow cat saw Tom
and the mountain coming close, it always
outwitted them. So they went on until
they came to the seaside, and there it
jumped into the arms of a mermaid.
And – disappeared entirely.

'May I borrow your rowing boat to go after the
mermaid who just catnapped my shadow?' Tom
asked, in too much of a hurry to notice there was
something fishy about the boatman. And Tom did not
see the mermaid push his boat out to sea, nor how she
hid his shadow in her hair.

Oh, yes – the moonshadow cat was full of tricks! Tom never knew when or where he would catch a glimpse of it next. It came and went with the movements of the sun, wind and waves and he could not catch it because catching a shadow with your bare hands is like trapping moonlight in a sieve.

Rowing was no fun. Soon Tom was tired and hot. Sea creatures tangled up his oars. When he saw a tropic isle, he thought: 'Time for a rest,' but nothing on the moonshadow cat quest was what it seemed.

No island, this! But a big bird of the parrot kind, most upset to be disturbed.

'Oh, Mr Parrot, don't eat me!' cried Tom. 'I'm only Tom in search of his shadow!' The sympathetic parrot flapped its wings and told Tom to hop aboard. So the moonshadow cat quest continued by air—over the sea, over the mountains where curious castles crouched… but Tom could not see his moonshadow cat anywhere because it was racing across the clouds above him.

They flew so far, so fast, so high, that Tom grew dizzy. His fingers skidded on the parrot's feathers. Help! He was falling!

Falling – falling so fast there was no time to be scared before he landed, plop, in a soft, dark place. A furry voice cooed: 'Who are you, my little roo?'

'I'm Tom in search of his shadow!' And where had Tom got to, now?

HE WAS BOUNDING ALONG IN A KANGAROO'S POUCH

'Stop!' cried Tom. 'I spy catprints!' The
Kangaroo was sure the prints looked too fierce for
those of a little moonshadow cat but Tom followed
them, all the same. He followed them and followed
them – until they led him right into the grin of a

TIGER!

'I say, do you like circuses?' inquired this friendly beast. Tom loved circuses even better than shadow games. The moment he saw the clowns, the bunting and the magnificence of the ringmaster, he forgot his moonshadow cat – but the moonshadow cat did not forget about Tom, even when it was sleeping.

What excitements! Tom stayed on the
back of the tiger all through the show.
He jumped through all the hoops with him
and the packed big top roared with glee and
clapped until their hands were sore.
'Well done, Tom!' said the ringmaster. 'But –
where is your shadow? Every boy should have
a shadow!' Once again, Tom told his story.

'You must consult the gypsy fortune-teller,' said the ringmaster. 'I'll take you to her caravan.'

The gypsy fortune-teller took out her crystal ball and started to look for the moonshadow cat in it. Then some sixth sense made Tom look up. There, behind the fortune-teller, was the biggest shadow he had ever seen and the shadow looked angry.

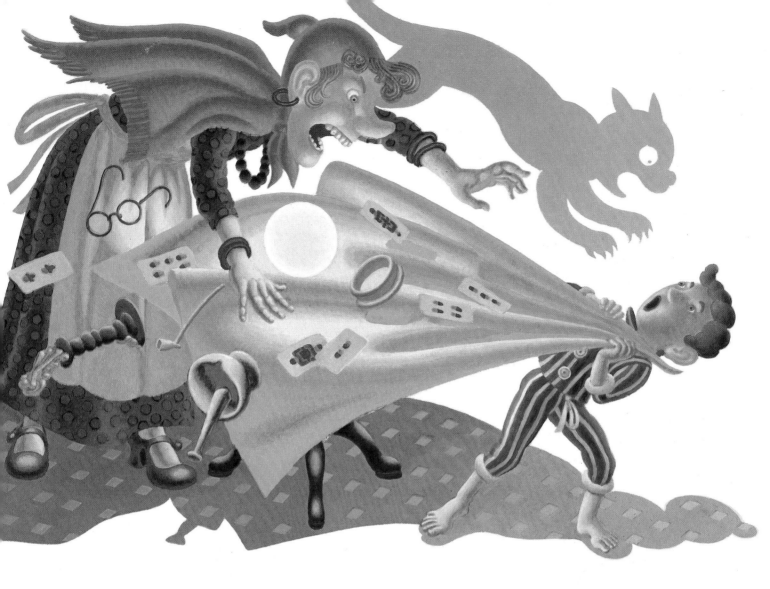

It was his very own moonshadow cat! But it did not
want its holiday to end. What? Turn back into a
common or garden boyshadow, always at Tom's beck
and call? It swelled with fury at the very thought.
Bigger, fiercer it grew, while the crystal ball glowed
on with more and more a bright, cold light until Tom
saw that, all the time, it had been the moon and then
– oh! – the moonshadow cat **JUMPED**.

And – ah! – here comes the Man in the Moon again!
'Time's up!' he screeched.

And that was that.

'Good morning,' said Mother. And there was Tom, safe in his own bed.

'Oh!' said Tom. 'I *did* have such a dream!' He told Mother all about it.

'Silly old thing,' said Mother. 'Fancy you being scared of your own shadow.'

'In future,' said Tom, 'I shall sleep soundly all through the night. If I don't play games with my shadow, then it won't play games with me!'

'Quite right,' said Mother.

The End

HITCH A RIDE
WITH A ROCK GIANT
AND GO TO 19

PLAY GAMES AT THE
CIRCUS AND GO BACK
TO 78

TAKE A BIG
FORWARD
ADVANCE T

The Rules of the Game
The Moonshadow Cat can race round
the course in 13 throws of a pair of dice.
Can you beat it?

P.S. This game can be played by
one person or more